GODS OF GANGES

Suraj Pratap

Fiction reveals truth that reality obscures.

This is a work of fiction.

Index

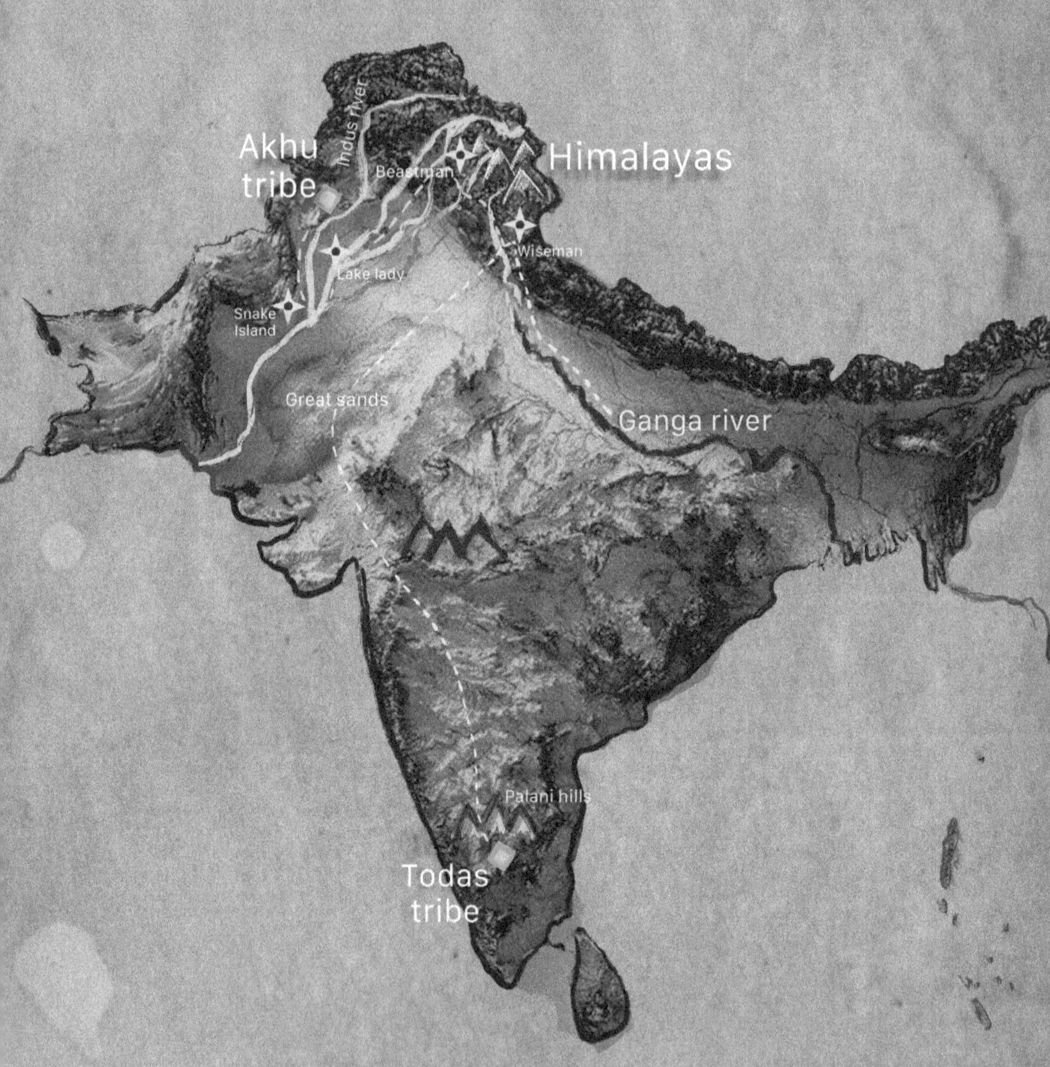

Akhu tribe
Himalayas
Indus river
Beastman
Wiseman
Lake lady
Snake Island
Great sands
Ganga river
Palani hills
Todas tribe

Chapter 1
Hunter-Gatherer

उप तवाग्ने दिवे-दिवे दोषावस्तर्धिया वयम |
नमो भरन्त एमसि ||

To thee, dispeller of the night, O Agni,

day by day with prayer, bringing thee reverence, we come.

(Rigveda 1:001:07)

Ten Thousand Years Ago.

The Indian subcontinent is a terrifying region, teeming with dangers created by both man and nature. This epoch, between the Neolithic and Copper ages, is a time when the world is grappling with challenges of unpredictable weather, deadly wildlife and brutal inter-tribal conflicts. Torrential rains, deadly storms, flash floods as well as seasonal droughts and wildfires make life difficult. Deadly predators that attack day and night and frequently target the very old and very young, pose a constant threat to survival. Furthermore, poor synchrony among tribes, cannibalistic traits, and inability to understand each other's languages and customs cause frequent friction between different groups often ending in carnage.

The Akhu Tribe is a small clan of fifty-two members: fourteen men, eighteen women, and twenty children. Situated in the Riwat Valley,[1] their village is daunting to outsiders due to its remote location, yet beautiful to its inhabitants. They are happy in their own small world. Tribe leader Eenali and his eldest son Emla, who is also his designated successor, lead a team of eight men out one morning for hunting and gathering.

Eenali has a spring in his step and hums his favorite tune as months of hard work have finally borne fruit. He

---

[1] Modern-day Punjab

is happy and content, and he dreams of a wonderful future for his family and tribe. *Things have been going well for a while*, he tells himself. Eenali's younger son, Ra, will also join the hunt today. It was not an easy task to get him to join. In fact, it has taken Eenali months to convince his wife to allow their youngest son to join the hunting missions. His wife remains terrified of the dangers that lurk in the wild. After all, her precious one is only 13 years old. But Eenali believes that Ra needs to learn the skills of survival in this formidable land, and now is the perfect time. It is never too early to be prepared, and he may very well need to take over from his brother and lead the tribe one day. Although his wife argued day and night, Eenali did not budge. He is determined to initiate Ra's training and teach him the art of being a hunter, leader, and fighter.

Eenali has been the leader of the tribe for seven years now. The tribe chose him out of desperation when the previous leader died in a tribal attack, but he has been very successful thus far. Eenali has proven his mettle by leading the tribe to prosperity. Under his guidance, the tribe has been able to gather food aplenty. Even the population has increased from just five huts to a prosperous twenty.

One might think that Eenali was lucky to find resources and survive the harsh winters. However, luck had nothing to do with his leadership. He has seen his fair share of pain. Within his first year of leadership, they had to relocate the tribe on two occasions. The

4

first was due to a massive flood that ravaged them for days. Then a savage attack by marauders occurred. The tribe lost many men and was forced to flee to less favorable locations.

Although things have been going well, the tribe's resources have been gradually diminishing, and so has the security of the village. The current location does not offer the safety net that they once enjoyed. Despite the village being surrounded by massive mountains on one side and thick woods on two other sides, it is partially exposed on one side.

Today, their team is venturing out to hunt a giant wild boar.[2] When they finally encounter a group of wild boars, they chase after them with their flint-tipped spears. Some of the strikes miss the mark, and others are often futile as their spear tips break on contact. Hunting is not easy. It takes years of practice and resources to become a master hunter.

Eenali's men are experienced, but they are no match for the quick and mighty boars. The spear tips of four hunters shatter in the process. Desperate, one of the men fashions a noose and throws it around the neck of a smaller boar. The boar, equally desperate to survive, drags him with all of its might. In the blink of an eye, the hunter has become the hunted. The man yells for help,

---

[2] Descendants of Daeodon

with panic taking over his features. Emla grabs him by the ankles and saves him just in time. However, before he can recover, the alpha boar charges directly into the team and stabs two men with its tusks, fatally injuring them. Emla sees the bloody clash and tries to intervene by shouting as loud as he can, hoping to distract the beast. His brave and timely action saves some of the teammates in the nick of time but he himself cannot escape and gets jabbed in the thigh.

Things are appearing bleak for the hunters, but their leader Eenali cannot imagine returning home empty-handed. *People at home must be hungry*, he reminds himself. He can sense his team's disappointment and his injured son's plight. Just as he tries to plan his next move, along comes another boar. Thankfully, this one is not as big as the previous one.

Eenali quickly pulls himself together and assesses the situation. Mother Nature has given him a second chance. He signals the uninjured hunters to split into two teams. Both teams attack together, offering no opportunity for the boar to retaliate. After what seems like hours, they finally capture and kill their prey.

The hunters immediately get to work and make arrangements to carry the boar home. During the return trip, Ra, inquisitive as ever, asks Eenali why they hunt with only seven to eight men.

"Wouldn't it be easier to hunt if we had more men?" Ra asks.

Smiling, Eenali ruffles his son's hair, finding it hard to believe that his son had grown up so quickly.

"True. There is strength in numbers, but we must be careful. Our safety is always at risk when we expose more men to danger," Eenali replies.

"How so?" Ra prods further.

"Well, what if someone attacks our village? We must leave some men back home to defend our families, right?"

Ra nods, understanding his father's words. Eenali remembers the last time they were attacked. Although they survived with very few casualties, the sudden attack made him realize that they could not take anything for granted.

The world was becoming increasingly difficult to live in. He glances at Emla, the future leader of the tribe. Limping and grimacing in pain, Emla would forever remember the boar and the lessons learned today.

Many young men in the tribe envy Emla and his injuries may further embolden conspirators, wonders Eenali. There is nothing Eenali can do about it. There are some aspects of leadership that can only be learned from experience.

Eenali uses this opportunity to remind his tribesmen that they must always remain vigilant if they want to survive. After all, there were two small attacks in the past month alone.

Upon returning to their land, they find that Eenali's words were truer than he had imagined. Their community has been decimated, and tribe members have been murdered. Only six women, five children, and one old man were able to survive the slaughter by hiding.

Horrified by the events that had unfolded in front of their eyes, the survivors tell the hunters that they were attacked by Calati marauders - a tribe from the Zagros Mountains. All of the huts have been burnt, and bodies litter the ground. Some of the young children were caught and taken away by Calatis as food.

Eenali's eyes desperately search for his wife amidst all the burning huts and rubble. Hoping against hope, he yearns for her, only to find her lifeless body lying in the ruin. Heartbroken, he weeps next to her bloodied body. Ra and Emla hold their mother's body closely, unable to control their tears.

Eenali's first thought is revenge, served immediately. He has half a mind to hunt down the monsters who killed his beautiful wife and little children. *Those bloodthirsty beasts must be taught a lesson*, his inner voice screams. However, his thoughts cease after one look at Ra.

The Calatis are cannibals. Encountering them will mean risking the lives of the remaining tribesmen, including

Emla and Ra. Moreover, Eenali reminds himself that he does not have the manpower to take on such a mission. Whatever was left of the tribe would be destroyed. "No," he tells himself, "We must escape now."

With great pain, he pushes the thought of revenge to the back of his mind and focuses on the tribe's future. He can think of nothing apart from his wife, but the tribe's safety is of the utmost importance. One wrong move and their tribe will be wiped from the face of the earth. He realizes that they must relocate once again, as this village is compromised and no longer safe. But where? They will need to find a location that will offer protection from invaders.

Eenali orders the tribe to bury their dead and pack any remaining essentials. Despite the grief tearing his heart apart, his tribe's safety is his responsibility. They hurriedly seek blessings from their ancestors at the half-destroyed village temple before embarking on a long, treacherous expedition.

However, it does not make sense to take off in an unknown direction without preparation, for it could be rife with predators of all sorts. Thus, Eenali decides to scout along the river with Emla and two other tribesmen to find a suitable location. The rest of the tribe follows in a caravan of men, women, children, donkeys, and goats.

Chapter 2
The Invisible Killer

अचिकित्वाञ्चिकितुषश्चिदत्र कवीन पर्छामि विद्मने न विद्वान |

वि यस्तस्तम्भ षळ इमा रजांस्यजस्य रूपे किमपि सविदेकम ||

I ask, unknowing, those who know, the sages,

as one all ignorant for sake of knowledge,

What was that One who in the unborn's image hath

stablished and fixed firm these worlds' six regions?

(Rigveda 1:164:06)

In Western Ghaat, the village of Todas tribe is tucked away deep in the Palani foothills.[3] Their village is a gorgeous community with serene, snow-capped mountains all around. The tribe members usually keep to themselves, but they sometimes venture northeast for exploration, following the river that flows across for hundreds of miles.

Elders of this tribe and neighboring villages often speak of an ancient legend: the Kingdom of the White Elephant. Village ancestors believe that the kingdom is sprawled atop the gigantic mountains amidst a thick blanket of snow. Meanwhile, the King and his followers possess knowledge and technology far more advanced than anywhere else in the Deccan Plateau. They can be identified by the legendary White Elephant. These beliefs are so strong and ancient that many tribal villages and temples are named after the "White Elephant" in their local languages.

The chief of the Todas tribe, Kiki, is an old man who has seen many seasons of ups and downs. The scars on his face recite countless stories of struggle and survival that go back decades. His tribe believes that he has the wisdom and experience to protect and lead them. Kiki is an exceptional thinker. Rather than attempting to compete, he has established friendly relationships with other tribe leaders. Following suit, the neighboring villages maintain

---

[3] Near modern-day Madurai

amicable relations rather than the hostility common in this era. Their coalitions increase their strength and ensure peace in the region.

The foothills of Palani offer ample resources for everyone. Todas tribe and neighboring entities rely on farming and fishing for sustenance; thus, they rarely need to hunt. The tribe leaders frequently gather to ensure friendly relations in the broader Vaigai region. Cultural mixing and coherence are encouraged, and they promote inter-tribal marriages and cultural festivals. They all live in a manner comparable to one big happy family. Moreover, the tribal elders know each other personally and share a deep sense of belonging.

The end of the monsoon season represents a time for celebrations, unions, and harvest. Men and women revel in joy, cherishing everything that Mother Nature offers. Lately, everyone has been happy and content, but their world was not always like this.

Kiki is well aware that his ancestors sacrificed much to ensure a golden future for the coming generations. Decades ago, the tribe's elders had traveled to the far north. It was the greatest of all quests, during which they learned advanced techniques to generate fire, make sophisticated tools for farming and domesticate cows. Upon their return, they were severely exhausted, and the crew had diminished in size; however, they appeared content because they could finally share the secrets that they had learned with their tribe.

From overcoming farming-related challenges to defending themselves from invaders, they passed tremendous knowledge to the next generation. Leaders that followed have been forever grateful to their ancestors and their great quest. They, in turn, have shared skills with neighboring tribes, and everyone has worked together to maintain peace and harmony.

Nevertheless, things are now changing rapidly. Certainly, they had learned skills to ward off invaders and reap bountiful harvests. They did not have to fear predators because they were relatively geographically safe. However, what could they possibly do about fatal illnesses? How could they fight an enemy that was invisible, yet omnipresent? Marsh fever has begun to wreak havoc on the tribe. Kiki and his contemporaries feel helpless as they could not do anything about it.

Kiki's forefathers had warned him about the plague of mosquitoes that afflicts people once every year. But once in many decades, the infestation is so severe that it can turn the evening sky dark before sunset. It is not known as the "harbinger of death" for nothing.

As fate would have it, the plague of their generation arrived just a few weeks after the harvest festival. Almost every family in the tribe has started to see several members suffering from the dreadful disease. Initially, the plague affects an individual with twice-weekly fevers. Without aid, it renders the individual debilitated and disoriented. Before long, their bellies bulge, and the color of their skin changes as well. Kiki knows how to identify sick individuals from their yellow eyes and skin, as he remembers all of the symptoms that his forefathers had described. However, this year, another sickness has been spreading concurrently. Beyond the deliriousness and yellow eyes, many tribesmen are suffering from severe debilitation, but without abdominal distension. Instead of their skin turning yellow, it is turning black. They appear so weakened as if they are about to collapse and die at any moment. After ample contemplation, Kiki realizes that he is dealing with a combination of Marsh Fever and Black Death. He feels a chill up his spine because his tribe is wholly unprepared for this deadly assault. The very future of their tribe is at stake.

Later that night, Kiki sees a group of black storks flying across the moonlit sky. He interprets it as a sign from his forefathers that he must step out of his comfort and do something different - something that will protect his people from deadly diseases and heal the community's broken morale. Unlike other leaders, Kiki is not one to curse fate. The time to worry has long gone; it is now time to act. He must act before these deadly epidemics swallow his tribe and spit them out like forgotten pages of history.

Accordingly, he decides to seek higher knowledge to ensure his tribe's survival. If his forefathers had pulled impossible feats generations ago, then he could do it as well.

He assembles his tribe members and addresses the meeting with the intention to reignite at least a little bit of optimism.

"My fellow tribesmen, the loss and tragedy we are suffering through is not hidden from anyone. We are mourning for our dead kin almost every other day. Our healers have been unable to find a cure for the double whammy of deadly diseases," Kiki pauses to ensure that he has the crowd's attention.

"As your leader, I can see both despair and a ray of hope in your eyes.

Today, I have called this gathering to assure you that either I will find a way out of this misery or I will die trying. Like you, I too am tired of burying our brothers and sisters. Like you, my heart also aches when I see children and newborns struggling with fever. And like you, I am also fed up with waiting for miracles. Remember, we are the descendants of the White elephant. We were not born to perish; we were born to persist. And persist we will!"

He realizes that his contemporaries have already given up all hope after seeing their families and friends dying day after day. However, he implores them to trust him. Kiki intends to wrestle his tribe out of the jaws of death, and he will not rest until he achieves his objective. Although the people are not wholly convinced, they sense Kiki's determination. They are scared, but they believe that Kiki at least has the motivation to seek a solution. After all, what choices do they have?

Satisfied that he has done his best to convey the message, Kiki calls for a meeting with neighboring tribal leaders, all of whom come hurriedly with their fighters in tow. They are as desperate as Kiki. Together, they decide to scout the region for more advanced tribes that may have medicinal knowledge to help them survive this epidemic.

Kiki's daughter Nira, an expert in map-making, asks to join the crew. Kiki resists but ultimately gives in after thinking about the future of his people.

Chapter 3

The Fireman

भवा मित्रो न शेव्यो घर्तासुतिर्विभूतद्युम्न एवया उ सप्रथाः |
अधा ते विष्णो विदुषा चिदर्ध्य सतोमो यज्ञश्चराध्यो हविष्मता ||

Far shining, widely famed, going thy wonted way,

fed with the oil, be helpful, *mitra*-like, to us.

O' Vishnu, e'en the wise must swell thy song of praise,

and he who hath oblations pay thee solemn rites.

(Rigveda 1:156:01)

In the northwest, Eenali and his tribesmen walk for seven days along the river. They travel carefully to avoid attracting the attention of other tribes, many of whom are known cannibals.

One day, they see a man wearing a saffron robe. He is surprisingly fearless, despite seeing a long caravan approaching. Looking at this lone man who is vulnerable yet unafraid gives Eenali some courage. He calmly introduces himself as the *messenger* and smiles as Eenali pours out his own troubles. Eenali befriends him and admits that he is fearful that their tribe will decline and might be eradicated.

"Well, if you want to offer any meaningful resistance to the invaders, you will need to increase your stock and strength of the weapons you're carrying. This way, you can at least hope to fight off your attackers," the messenger says.

Eenali agrees but does not know how to go about doing so. "There is a man who lives at the intersection of streams, where the five rivers meet," the messenger says, sensing Eenali's trepidation. "His rock castle is guarded by fire, and he sleeps on a bed of snakes. He and his consort know all weaponry and are capable of creating weapons out of the ground. Their magical powers are known all across the region. If you find him and seek his help, you may stand a chance, provided that the *Fireman* is willing to teach you some of his magical skills."

Eenali ponders over the messenger's words. He shudders at the thought of a man sleeping on a bed of snakes. He hesitates because it seems quite risky. He glances at the wounded Emla, who appears to be thinking the same. Emla finds the story fascinating but asks his father if it is worth traveling so far and risking the lives of the tribesmen for some myth. However, Eenali knows that they will need to take this chance. After all, it is either now or never.

Eenali thanks the messenger for his advice, and with grim determination, the tribe continues treading carefully along the river.

The Fireman lives in a cave situated on a stony island that is located in the delta formed by the confluence of five rivers. There are two pyres on each side of the entrance, with fires that are contained, yet more intense than any fire that Eenali has ever seen. Eenali's group steps onto the island and passes through the giant entrance. Inside the circular, castle-like island is a cave with a retractable wooden bridge as the only way to enter.

"The bridge is pulled up which means we will have to pass through the moat," Eenali observes.

The tribe is initially hesitant to proceed, but Eenali asks them to carefully scout the entire area. The moat around the cave is filled with poisonous snakes.

"I think I see a potential passage through the moat," says a brave tribesman.

"Tread quietly and be very careful, I will use my vantage point to alert you If I see any danger," replies Eenali while giving him the permission to proceed.

Eenali and his tribesmen hold their breath as they watch their friend quietly sneak through a moat full of snakes. Just when they feel he might reach the other end he steps on a brown snake that was so well hidden in the sand that it was impossible to see it. The brave tribesman writhes in pain and shock as the snake bites his leg. As he falls back, hundreds of snakes attack him and the poor man dies a painful death.

After struggling for two days and losing one of their men to the snakes, Eenali is almost ready to quit. He feels incredibly guilty that he was the one who had brought them here. However, just when it seems as though all hope is lost, the Fireman comes out of his stone castle and looks at the tribesmen.

Eenali folds his hands together in a gesture of respect. He hopes desperately that the Fireman will take them under his wings, as they have no other options. Several minutes later, the wooden bridge descends, allowing them to enter the Fireman's kingdom.

Fireman had just returned after an expedition to a nearby village. There is a secret passage that he uses to enter and exit the island. Looters were torturing the villagers for months before the village elders came to the Fireman for help. Using his unparalleled battle skills and advanced weapons, the Fireman easily defeated the gang of tormentors and killed their top three leaders to drive his message home: no oppression will be tolerated in the Fireman's country.

He is still wearing his battle armor made of plates of hardened material weaved in an overlapping design that amazes the tribesmen. Eenali and others gaze at the Fireman in awe. They have never encountered anyone like him; he has a long, sharp sword that would intimidate even the most savage attackers, and he wears a crown with a face shield, which is protective and magnificently intimidating.

The Fireman gives Eenali and his group shelter and teaches them an array of skills. First, he teaches them how to create a sustainable fire. Next, he trains them how to create sturdy tools. Like a sponge, Eenali and his tribesmen absorb everything that he teaches.

The Fireman offers them several pieces of pyrite rocks that can be used with flint strikers to create fire quickly through friction.

"There is a large source of such rocks in the south,[4] and the hills in that area are inhabited by an advanced tribe that I had once mentored," he tells them.

He also teaches them to initiate fire using tinder and fat and to preserve fire by using burnt wood as a base. The Fireman then gives them seeds of emmer wheat and demonstrates how to grow them. The men also learn how to crush the seeds into a powder that is easy to store and serves as a good source of food when mixed with water and cooked in fire.

Eenali notices that the Fireman spends many hours every day producing very intense fires. He uses it in specially designed kilns to melt stones.[5] The Fireman tells Eenali that these are special stones with a greenish hue and teaches him how to distinguish them from other stones in nature. The Fireman then beats the molten stones into precise shapes to create the strongest weapons and armor that Eenali has ever seen. Pleased with their eagerness to grasp knowledge, the Fireman gifts some of his special swords, spears, and arrowheads made of molten rock to them.

Lastly, the Fireman's companion shows the tribe how to identify the Karpasa,[6] which produces a peculiar type of fibrous material. What fascinates Eenali and his men is that the material can be threaded and used to make fabric for clothes.

---

[4] Deccan plateau

[5] Copper ore

[6] Gossypium plant

These clothes offer much better protection and warmth than the traditional leaves or dried animal skin to which they have been accustomed. The Fireman gives Eenali two sets of armor made of intricately woven pangolin scales. They may not be as strong as the Fireman's shiny armor, but they are lighter and offer much better protection and flexibility than the leather that Eenali's tribesmen have been using.

Eenali says, "Oh, Savior, you have taught us invaluable skills. You were very kind to us and helped us when we had lost all hope. I do not know how to thank you. But the time to leave your island has come. We shall now bid farewell as we are better prepared for the brutal world out there."

The Fireman smiles and replies, "I believe that you are not as prepared as you may think. I suggest you seek the guidance of the *Beastman*."

The Fireman tells Eenali that he had taught them the Secret of Fire, the Secret of Water, and the Secret of Earth, but that they needed to learn the Secret of Life in order to truly be successful.

Nevertheless, Eenali's tribe has already dwindled too significantly to take additional risks. The weight on his chest has just doubled as he once again wonders if it is worth the risk. After all, it was a major challenge to reach the Fireman. The Fireman and his consort allow the tribesmen to stay near their castle for a full moon. Emla is now partially healed and walks using a crutch.

Despite Eenali's hesitation, the Fireman tries to be honest with him. He explains that they must travel north to reach the Beastman. Eenali is quietly listening, wondering how to respond. He is not certain that they have the strength to start another challenging journey, considering how his tribe is dwindling quickly.

"It won't be easy by any means," the Fireman notes before adding, "but there is a lutenist who knows a quicker and less dangerous route. Follow me."

The Fireman then leads Eenali to the highest rock on the delta and points to a lake. "The musician resides somewhere there."

"But how will we identify her?" questions Eenali.

"Look for swans and listen for chimes," the Fireman answers enigmatically. "If you're successful, you will find the *Lady of the Lake*."

Eenali leads his tribe up the stream. After walking for two days, they come across a lake full of beautiful white swans and cranes. As Eenali and his tribesmen proceed toward the lake, a group of large swans attacks them with such ferocity that the tribe is forced to pause. Eenali knows there is no turning back.

Chapter 4
Elephant King

पर हि करतुं वर्हथो यं वनुथो रध्रस्य सथो यजमानस्य चोदौ ।
इन्द्रासोमा युवमस्मानविष्टमस्मिन भयस्थे कर्णुतमु लोकम ॥

Whomso ye love, his power ye aid and strengthen;

ye twain are the sincere worshipper's advancers.

Graciously favour us, Indra and Soma; give us firm

standing in this time of danger.

(Rigveda 02:030:06)

In the Deccan Plateau, Kiki and his team finally find a smooth, uphill passage that starts along the edges of the Palani Hills. Tribe leaders have exhausted all alternatives, and despite no guarantee of any advanced kingdom upon the hill, this seems to be their only option. The terrain becomes increasingly dangerous the farther up the hill they go. Even if such a kingdom does exist, it will have strong defenses and its guards could kill Kiki's expedition at first sight. Despite the gamble, Kiki is willing to take that risk for the future of his tribe and those who live nearby.

After trekking through the forest, water, and heavy snowfall, the group encounters large footprints that resemble those of an elephant. Excited, they scout the area but fail to find the legendary creature. The stories that had been passed on for generations describe it as a beautiful white animal covered in splendid, colorful stones. Legend also has it that the majestic animal wears a beautiful saddle for the king.

A brief discussion among the leaders provides them with the necessary motivation for the final stretch. After another two-day long trek, they finally see a large wooden gate with beautiful designs and an ice wall around it. The tribe finds a way to cross over the ice wall and finally gain a glimpse of the fabled elephant. They had reached the Kingdom of White Elephant.

Slightly larger than the Indian elephant, this albino variant has four large tusks.[7] From atop the wall they notice the settlement, composed primarily of huts made of wood and ice. They realize the lack of mosquitoes and other parasites in the kingdom, in large part due to the cold and altitude. Despite the snow, there are carefully cultivated areas where crops, fruits, and mushrooms are growing.

"It must have taken a lot of planning, but everything is simply perfect," wonders Kiki.

He and his men have heard tales of the White Elephant, but nothing could prepare them for its splendor. Enthralled by its magnanimous tusks, they fail to notice the dozens of guards quietly surrounding them. The guards capture them and take them to their king.

---

[7] Descendent of Gomphothere

The *Elephant King* is a giant of a man with a chiseled body. At a towering six-and-a-half feet tall, his arms look like thick intertwined ropes. The armor on his chest blazes like fire, and his bejeweled crown has a metallic sheen, enough to blind spectators. Meanwhile, his ornate cape moves as though it has a mind of its own. He also wears metallic leg wraps and sandals and carries a glistening white dagger that looks like a hefty amalgamation of bone and metal with a sharp pointed tip. Contrary to Kiki's fears, the Elephant King is forgiving toward the trespassers.

"My lord, we have traveled for days and faced countless dangers to see you. Our families

and tribes are being ravaged by epidemics. Would you be so kind as to share some of your knowledge? Your generosity might give us a chance to endure the brutal onslaught of diseases," Kiki asks with his hands joined together as a gesture of respect.

"Your determination and bravery are commendable. We will help you."

Kiki sighs a breath of relief when the Elephant King states that he will share some of his knowledge with them. Sensing that they must return home soon, the Elephant King begins meeting them for several hours each day. He confides in them that he was taught weaponry skills and forging techniques by the legendary Fireman of the north.

First, he hands Kiki some lemon grass,[8] which can be used to deter parasites. Then he gives them the fruits of *Bhumiamla*[9] as protection against jaundice before teaching them how to identify these plants in the wild.

The Elephant King also directs his cooks to show them non-conventional foods, such as oyster mushrooms,[10] which can be dried and stored for later use. They can also be seeped and boiled to prepare a very potent analgesic.

---

[8] Indian citronella
[9] Phyllanthus niruri
[10] Pleurotus pulmonarius

After learning valuable lessons from Elephant King for three days, Kiki and his squad plan to leave on a clear morning to avoid any mishaps. The journey downhill could be treacherous; however, his motivated teammates are prepared to take on the next challenge. Nevertheless, the Elephant King cautions them not to leave since a major rainstorm is expected at any time. He assures them that he will teach them many more lifesaving skills over the next several days of their stay.

Kiki and his men look at the clear sky and wonder why the Elephant King predicts otherwise. Much to their surprise, it begins pouring heavily within a few hours, as predicted by the Elephant King.

Emboldened by the generosity that the Elephant King has bestowed thus far, Kiki requests him to share some meteorological secrets. The Elephant King explains that over the past many decades, by observing the weather, and by virtue of the altitude of the region, he has mastered the art of weather prediction.

"Of course, it will take years before you master it, but it's never too late to start," he comments with a smile.

"I am a good student," responds Kiki.

The Elephant King, pleased with Kiki's desire to learn, decides to share some basic rules, such as the density of the fog and the importance of the halos around the sun.

The following day, the Elephant King asks his cook to teach them the method of preparing curd from milk and fermenting jackfruit into wine. He offers them a map to lead them to the location where major sources of knowledge emanate: the Himalayas.

The Elephant King then tells them that their trek up the Palani Hills is just a starter. It has now primed them for their real objective, which is the journey that lies ahead. He wishes them good luck. Pointing to the *Dhruv Tara,*[11] he explains that it always remains at the same point in the sky and will guide them in the right direction.

This is it, Kiki thinks.

The time has finally come for the brave few to step out of their quarters and embark on the second great quest for their tribe. The Elephant King provides the tribesmen spears with hardened, bright pink and blue tips made of corundum. Although they look different from the spears and swords used by the king's guards and the king himself, they are much stronger than anything that Kiki has ever seen. Kiki offers his thanks to the Elephant King and embarks on the expedition to the Far North. The Elephant King promises to use his vantage point and knowledge of meteorology to light his giant fire pyres as a signal to alert the downhill tribes of any incoming storm while their leaders are away.

----

[11] Pole Star

Chapter 5

Lady of the Lake

चोदयित्री सूत्रतानां चेतन्ती सुमतीनाम |

यज्ञं दधे सरस्वती ||

Inciter of all pleasant songs, inspirer of all gracious thoughts,

Sarasvati accept our rite.

(Rigveda 1:003:11)

Eenali and his tribesmen are finally able to break into the outer circumference of the lake surrounded by white and gray swans. He sees a woman clad in a white robe standing outside a hut on a tiny island in the middle of the lake.

"The Lady of the Lake," mumbles Eenali. A circular raft is also tied there. The woman is feeding a majestic swan,[12] bigger than any swan Eenali has ever seen.

The woman and Eenali notice each other from afar, and the swan immediately flies toward Eenali's group. It is a giant of an animal, and it flaps its wings with such ferocity that the terrified tribesmen hide for cover.

When the swan flies away, Eenali comes out, joins his hands together, and bows to the woman on the island. She sees the gesture of respect and makes a sound from a tiny conch. The giant swan immediately calms down. She then begins playing her lute made of dried gourds.

The music is so soothing that the tribesmen take it as a message to stay. However, it is actually a message to a couple of swans that swim toward the group. To Eenali's surprise, they push the small raft. Eenali is hesitant to engage with the swans but realizes that they have come in peace.

After a quick glance at each other to indicate that it is safe, Eenali and Emla enter the boat. The boat is constructed

---

[12] Descendent of Cygnus falconeri

of only lotus leaves, but it does a splendid job carrying them to the hut in the middle of the lake. The Lady of the Lake is stunningly beautiful, with a subtle red blush on her cheeks and long, intricately braided hair. She is wearing a white saree with blue-lined edges and looks divine with the reflection of dew from the nearby lotuses.

Eenali folds his hands once again, enthralled with her mere presence.

"Can you please show us the route to the Beastman?" he asks.

She glances down at the two rivers in the valley below, clearly visible from the lake.

She smiles. "Just follow the river to your right, all the way upstream until the land turns icy white. Eventually, you will reach a distinct-looking mountain with black and white horizontal markings. That is where the Beastman lives."

Eenali nods.

"However, I must warn you," she adds. "The path is precarious. You will have to pass through dense forests filled with deadly beasts. The entire stretch of land is teeming with wild animals like giant tigers,[13] bears,[14]

---

[13] Descendants of Smilodons
[14] Descendants of Arctotherium

rhinoceros[15] as well as aquatic predators.[16] I suggest that you tread quietly and store food wherever you find it. My disciples will teach you how to identify clay-like material and mold it into pottery."

Eenali is grateful that the woman is willing to teach them survival skills. Handing over some special blueberries[17] to Eenali, she says enigmatically, "These berries will be very useful for you." She smiles and adds, "If you see local tribes wearing blue beads, it's your cue that you're very close to your destination."

"Take these Indigo leaves[18] as well," she adds, handing a basket full of leaves to Eenali. "Make sure that you save them. They will help you dye any fabric a vibrant blue."

"Dye? How do we do that?" questions Eenali. Nevertheless, he immediately wonders whether they are asking too much of her. "May I ask you to teach us?" he asks.

"Here, let me show you," she says. The woman proceeds to give him a brilliant-blue scarf. Eenali and his men are mesmerized by the color. Until now, Eenali only knew of one way to obtain a natural blue color, and that was through mining.

Mining is one of the most difficult tasks to perform, not to mention that it can be fatal after a period of time. Eenali

---

[15] Descendants of Coelodonta

[16] Descendants of Deinosuchus and Otodus auriculatus

[17] Elaeocarpus ganitrus

[18] Indigofera tinctoria

thinks about the men who lost their lives trying to mine blue stones. For reasons unbeknownst to them, it was rare that any blue stone miner lived beyond a couple of decades. One would think that the results would be spectacular, considering the immense effort that goes into it. However, after a laborious process, the final product was just a dirty-blue shade. The color produced by the blue stones was nothing compared to this masterpiece.

"You'll see a small hamlet as you proceed," the woman shares, flicking her hand in the route's direction. "I've taught the villagers to process the dye using these leaves. They will teach you the art of dying clothes as well as pottery."

Eenali struggles to contain his happiness. The woman has been very generous. He imagines that after they establish their new village, they can use the blue dye to trade for essential commodities.

"Use the blue fabric that I gave you to enter the Beastman's territory. The tribes in that area are very protective and will attack outsiders unless they see flags with this shade of blue."

Eenali and his tribesmen thank her profusely once again.

They all proceed to the hamlet as directed by the Lady of the Lake to rest for a couple of days. They stay in small, yet neat huts, thanks to the accommodating villagers. Over the next two days, the villagers teach them everything that they know about extracting blue color from the leaves.

Eenali watches the villagers pour the fermented mixture of leaves into a large container. They combine the mixture thoroughly with wooden paddles.

"We mix it so that air enters the mixture," the villager explains. "Once the liquid settles at the bottom of the container, we drain it with thick fabric and make a paste out of it. Finally, the paste is dried and powdered, after which it is ready to be used as a dye."

Eenali and his men hang on to every word that they hear. Little by little, they realize that they are truly advancing into a better tribe. Eenali is glad that there is still hope for his men. He has had his fair share of doubts regarding whether they would even survive.

Before their departure, The Lady of the Lake visits them in the hamlet and shows a unique symbol of four lines around a circle.[19] "Once you see this symbol, you will have arrived at your destination," she says.

At last, she bestows a whistle-like instrument that produces a high-pitched sound with which the tribesmen can identify each other if they get separated or are lost in the forests. Eenali and his tribe bow to her as a gesture of respect and begin their journey onward.

---

19 Early Swastika

Chapter 6
Stars and Shadows

स घा नो योग आ भुवत स राये स पुरन्ध्याम् ।
गमद वाजेभिरा स नः ॥

May he stand by us in our need,

and in abundance of our wealth.

May he come nigh us with his strength.

(Rigveda 1:005:03)

In the south, Kiki and his team are about to embark on the difficult journey ahead to the northern ice by following the Pole Star. Before leaving, they pay one final visit to their tribes and share their knowledge about medicinal herbs and corundum. Slowly, the tribes build confidence that Kiki and his team may make it and what initially seemed like a hopeless mission might have enormous value. Kiki has confidence in his abilities and team, but he also recognizes that they might not come back. Despite the inevitable dangers that they are about to face, Kiki is determined to do as much as he can for his people. Still, Kiki is not a man who counts his victories before the end of a journey. Kiki and his men pray one final time to their tribe's deities and hope that the herbs and stronger weapons will protect their tribe until they return. With a heavy heart, they bid them farewell.

Kiki's daughter, Nira, again requests to join the expedition, but Kiki is hesitant. He knows that she is physically and mentally capable, and he is aware that she is famous for her mapping skills. However, the father in him does not want to see his 17-year-old daughter in any kind of danger. He refuses steadfastly, but Nira persists.

"I'm your daughter, and I want to save our people, just like you," she says, stubbornly.

Ultimately, Kiki gives in because he knows deep down in his heart that they need every expert they can find. Her addition to the expedition can greatly increase their likelihood of survival and success. Everyone is elated to hear that Nira is joining the expedition.

The team embarks with great enthusiasm and hopes that they can achieve their objectives but over the next several days, they encounter a variety of wild animals. From poisonous snakes to leopards and boars, the tribesmen fight them all. They overcome many predators that they encounter but it comes at a price, they suffer multiple casualties. At this point, Kiki insists on prioritizing a stealthy approach and covering their tracks. Predators have a knack for noticing tracks and hunting down their prey. They cannot afford to lose more men. For days, the men travel without any hassles. Some of them feel a sense of relief, thinking that the worst is over; however, they unexpectedly find themselves at odds with a beast that few have been able to survive, the Giga Tiger.[20]

The Giga tiger is feared not just by humans, but also by other animals. Unsurprisingly, the predator is the king of the jungle. It traverses forests with ease, quickly grabbing prey to satisfy its insatiable hunger. What makes it so powerful and unbeatable is its agility, which defies its size. Unlike other animals that hunt in packs, the Giga tiger hunts alone. Although this may be an advantage

---

[20] Descendant of Smilodon

for some, it did not offer comfort to Kiki and his men. Perhaps, if it had hunted alongside its kinship, they may have heard them coming. But, then again, the Giga tiger is a master of camouflage. Even other animals are unaware of its presence in the shadows until it is too late.

Kiki had only heard of the ferocious beast from their ancestors. He knew that it would be enormous and ready to kill, but nothing had prepared him for this behemoth creature that was at least ten times the size of a regular human. The tribesmen, even if they unite and fight together, have no chance. Despite having strong weapons, Kiki knows that the Giga tiger could kill them all. Kiki stares at the beast from afar, and a chill creeps up his spine. It is just 5 feet in height, but it made up for it with its massive weight, weighing over five hundred kilograms. "It has fangs longer than my hand," thinks Kiki. Its smoldering green eyes are shining like giant emeralds. One strike of his powerful paw is enough to kill a man instantly. Kiki and his men have no idea what to expect. The beast had been following their group for many days, unbeknownst to the gullible tribesmen.

"How could we have missed such a giant creature?" wonders Kiki. Just as their caravan is about to cross the deep forests of modern-day Satpura, it is ambushed. One unsuspecting tribesman who was walking closest to the Giga tiger is instantly mauled to death before the others can even register what is happening.

With an ear-shattering roar enough to make them all deaf, the beast attacks another man and kills him by slashing his neck with his razor-sharp claws. The rest of the tribesmen watch in horror and amazement as the beast bites another man on the neck and then crushes his head by its powerful jaw within seconds.

Kiki looks the beast in its eyes and shouts as loudly as he can. As others gather their wits, they shout in unison, declaring to the beast that they are together. Kiki orders his men to attack the beast from all sides, as there is no way to escape except a fight to the death. The men form a team and attack the Giant tiger, but it still manages to injure five more men in succession. The tribesmen battle with the beast for almost ten minutes before realizing that they were losing their numbers as well as morale while the beast was attacking with even more strength. With no other means of escape, Kiki orders his men to retreat to a narrow cave. Nira had sighted this cave just in time and suggested to her father that hiding may be their best chance as the beast cannot enter the cave due to its gigantic size. Thinking quickly, Nira lights a couple of torch fires to startle and deter the beast.

The men huddle next to one another, scared for their lives. Although they are not cowards by any means, facing the deadly beast seems like suicide. Kiki prays that the beast becomes bored and departs, but it takes two days for it to finally leave.

Kiki takes a good look at his injured men. One of them dies after fighting for his life for two days. Nevertheless,

Kiki knows that they cannot stop now. Ordering the group to march forward, Kiki and his men silently leave the cave and continue until they reach the Malwa Plateau[21].

The Smilodon is nowhere to be seen, but the group is not taking any chances. They must avoid any dense foliage and forests. Nira comes up with a plan to travel along the Great Sands[22]. Kiki and his men turn to her in astonishment. How had she known about it? Despite being so young, Nira had learned about the Great Sands from some of her explorer friends, but no one from her own tribe knew about it.

"It will be difficult," she admits, facing the men. "We will have to weather the arid climate and scorching sun. Compared to the Great Sands, the jungles will seem like heaven because the scorching heat will burn our skin."

The men look at her in anticipation. "But," she continues, "we've been through the jungles. It is a miracle that we are even alive. Yes, the Great Sands are hot and dry, but deadly predators won't come there."

The men nod in response, and Kiki makes his decision: they will take their chances in the Great Sands before losing more of their men to deadly predators.

---

[21] Near modern-day Shipra River
[22] Modern-day Thar Desert

Chapter 7

The Long Journey

जानत्यह्णः परथमस्य नाम शुक्रा कष्णादजनिष्ट शवितीची |
रतस्य योषा न मिनाति धामाहर अहर्निष्क्रतमाचरन्ती ||

She who hath knowledge of the first day's nature is born

refulgent white from out the darkness.

The Maiden breaketh not the law of Order, day by day

coming to the place appointed.

(Rigveda 01:123:09)

Thousands of miles northwest, Eenali and his tribesmen have been walking for weeks. They save food whenever possible, as instructed by the Lady of the Lake. They are careful not to attract attention or pose a threat to other tribes.

The wild animals do not bother them and stay away for the most part - except for one fateful morning when they cross paths with the Colossal Monitor lizard[23] just before dawn.

At first, the tribesmen do not see it. However, Eenali's instincts warn him, and he senses that something is wrong, very wrong. A pungent odor fills the air, and he soon sees something from the corner of his eye. Behind several large bushes, he notices something blinking. It appears like a blazing red ruby but is much larger than his fist. Just as he wonders what it could be, the nightmarish reptile appears.

In shock, Eenali realizes that he has been staring at the Monitor lizard's eye. There is a collective gasp from the tribesmen as they have never seen anything like it. Huge is an understatement. Eenali notices that the reptile is at least 20 feet long and easily weighs more than 600 kilograms. It is a gigantic lizard, more like a dragon, ready to slay anyone brave enough to breathe in front of it.

The Giant lizard takes one step forward with its mighty limbs built like rock pillars. The tribesmen feel as though the earth is trembling.

____

[23] Descendant of Megalania

"Or is it our legs trembling?," Eenali wonders. The Monitor lizard hisses in anger, furious that the tribesmen have disturbed its peace in the quiet jungle. Of course, the tribesmen were not loud, but the Giant Lizard never appreciates having intruders in its homeland. The beast's head resembles a large mountain rock. The scales covering its body are rough, gross, and intimidating. As it roars, spreading terror in the hearts of the tribesmen, Eenali notices that its fangs are long enough to pierce his skull through and through. Even worse, they are more poisonous than some of the deadliest snakes in the world. With hundreds of yellow teeth lined inside its mouth, the Colossal Monitor lizard looks every bit ready for the kill.

It flicks its tongue out menacingly, like a cobra about to strike, but the only difference is that it is a thousand times bigger and deadlier than a snake. Its tail is magnificent, yet deadly enough to kill anyone with one blow. If that is not enough, it has claws sharper than the spears that Eenali and his team are carrying.

"It would take at least twenty men to tire this beast out," Eenali thinks, planning his next move. However, they do not have twenty men. For the hundredth time, Eenali wishes that he had never taken his tribesmen out to face a predator like this.

The animal takes a look at the tribesmen. Without warning, it swipes its tail, violently whipping a man's chest. The blow is so severe that the man is thrown many feet back. Another teammate helps the injured man stand up not

realizing that the Giant Lizard had quickly crawled up to the spot. Before the two can be alerted, the lizard bites one man's neck and then coils around the second who had not fully recovered from the blow. Both victims die - first due to poisoning and second due to suffocation. The rest of the tribesmen stare at its brutality, as if in a trance.

"Attack!" Eenali screams, pushing his men into action.

Pandemonium ensues. The men struggle to corner the beast, but it spews venom relentlessly, killing more of them in the process.

Emla realizes that there is no other way to kill it, other than aiming for its eye. Every beast has a soft spot on its skull. That is how the tribesmen once subdued a hostile rhinoceros when it was destroying their huts. He orders his teammates to retreat so that they can form a plan. Hastily, they agree with his decision as the beast advances toward them, angrier than ever.

The plan is to distract the Megalania and kill it by striking in the eye. The confidence with which Emla presents his plan, fills his father with pride. At first, two men run in front of the beast, close but not so close that it can attack. They must be far enough to defend themselves from the venom.

As the lizard chases them, Eenali and two other tribe members attack it from the side with sharp spears.

Despite being partially crutch dependent, Emla uses this opportunity to get very close to the lizard, as there is no other way to strike it. As the beast takes a moment to comprehend what is going on, Emla utters a prayer, takes aim, and hurls his spear right into the center of its skull.

The Colossal monitor lizard roars with all of its might, shaking tremendously. The men run for cover. However, just as it seems like the beast is about to attack them, it crashes into the ground, raising gusts of dust everywhere. The tribesmen cheer happily, as they have conquered the mammoth dragon. They gather around Emla and raise him on their shoulders, hailing his bravery and quick wit. However, Eenali is in no mood for celebration, as his caravan has further dwindled in size.

Shaken by the incident, the group becomes extremely discreet, trying its best not to attract attention. They are aware that another attack from a big predator will annihilate them. They continue treading in the directed path until the air turns icy and the land turns white. This is the milestone that the Lady of the Lake had told them about. They decide to halt for several days to recuperate from the long journey.

One morning, a tribesman from Eenali's group goes to a nearby lake[24], to fetch clean water. He comes across a

____

[24] Modern day Chandratal

beautiful woman who is also fetching water for drinking. Mesmerized by her beauty, he approaches her and grasps her arm. The woman glares at him, her eyes warning him to leave her alone. However, drunk with power, the tribal man tries to pull her closer. In a quick flash, the woman pulls a spike from her hair and stabs him in the arm. The tribesman stares at her, unable to comprehend what has just occurred. Before he can defend himself, the woman stabs him in the eye. Crying in excruciating pain, he immediately runs away to save his life.

Chapter 8

The Beastman

गाथपतिं मेधपतिं रुद्रं जलाषभेषजम |

तच्छंयोः सुम्नमीमहे ॥

To Rudra Lord of sacrifice, of hymns and balmy medicines,

We pray for joy and health and strength.

(Rigveda 01:043:04)

The remainder of the Eenali's tribe tries desperately to save their strongest companion who is gravely injured. They venture to the nearby village waving the blue flag and try to search for a doctor, but the villagers refuse to help them. After fruitlessly asking for help for hours, Eenali finally approaches a village elder.

"Do none of your villagers have any compassion left? I implore you to show some mercy. My caravan is on the verge of extinction. Our friend has been poisoned and his condition is deteriorating by the hour. Please help me find a cure or just tell me what type of poison it could be?," pleads distraught Eenali.

"The question is not what but who," replies the Elder.

"What do you mean?," Eenali is in no mood for riddles.

"The woman your friend tried to attack was none other than the Beastman's consort. They are masters of alchemy and make their own poisons as well as antidotes. Even if some villager has a faint idea, they will never share it with you. They are our God and Goddess. Our lives literally depend on them."

Once again Eenali feels as if fate has closed another door for him. The village elder explains to Eenali that Beastman is the only one who can command the power of the sun and create a sustainable fire in this icy terrain. In fact, he is merciful enough to visit small villages like theirs every few weeks to reignite the fires. Their village's central pyre was extinguished 3 days ago, and they have not been able to cook food or defend from predators. Their young children have been sleeping hungry and an old woman was snatched away by a snow leopard the previous night. They desperately need the Beastman so that the village fire can be reignited. He has always helped the residents of this valley and the villagers have faith that he will come soon.

Hearing the Elder's devotion to the Beastman, Eenali curses his luck. After everything that they have endured, one of his men had to torment a woman. Why could he not control his urges? Moreover, of all the women in the world, he had chosen the Beastman's consort.

It was Eenali's and the villagers' fortune that the Beastman came early next morning riding his Yak driven cart. His muscular arms and legs are obviously visible despite the bear skin and fur cape he is wearing. He brings with him a giant curved piece of ice which is almost as big as the cartwheel itself, hanging between two wooden planks. He carefully places it between the sun and the pyre and within minutes the fire is reignited due to the ice acting as a spherical lens. Eenali, who is quietly observing everything from the crowd, cannot help but join the villagers when they cheer for the Beastman – their savior, their god.

He realizes that the only way to save his friend's life now is to go to the Beastman's cave and ask for forgiveness.

But will the Beastman help him after hearing that his friend had misbehaved with his consort?

Nevertheless, Eenali has no choice. They cannot compromise their objective because of one man's blunder. The least that he can do is appeal to the Beastman that the mistake will not be repeated. If they were lucky, the Beastman would spare their lives.

Having made up his mind, Eenali leads his tribe along the mountain as directed by locals. After walking for one day, they finally approach the pinnacle of modern-day Gangotri Valley and find a castle-styled cave composed of stones and surrounded by two stone pyres. He sees the symbol that the lake lady showed him, carved on a giant rock.

They find a skinned white tiger sprawled on the ground at the entrance. The tribesmen look at one another in fear, wondering what they have gotten themselves into. They are now at the mercy of the Beastman.

As they enter the cave, they see a tall, muscular, dark-complexioned man holding a three-pointed spear. He has long hair braids with a top bun and a brilliant, blue-smeared neck. He wears the skin of a Giga tiger on his body, with its head forming the Beastman's shoulder armor - a testament to the fact that he has conquered the beast long ago. There is also a chain of human skulls around his waist, warning strangers not to get too close to him. He has a long bow behind his back, longer than any bow that Eenali has ever seen.

Eenali and his men stare at the formidable Beastman. He is the most handsome man that they have ever seen, yet the deadliest. His eyes blaze with fury, and his strong, ripped arms clutch a spear that must weigh at least fifty kilos. His thighs resemble perfectly shaped rocks, ready to travel long distances or kill someone with a mere kick. Meanwhile, the Beastman's chest is broad and chiseled. His mere presence spells power, and the tribesmen feel a mixture of awe and fear.

"If there is a God, the Beastman fits that description perfectly," thinks Eenali. He and the remaining tribesmen kneel in front of the Beastman and his consort in reverence. For them, the Beastman is nothing short of their master - the omnipresent, erudite being who can teach them everything that they need. "Now, he will probably order his men to kill us," shudders Eenali. He was afraid of meeting the legend due to the stories that he had heard, but now that he was in front of the man himself, he felt as though it was the final day of his life.

However, contrary to their fears, the Beastman does not look furious. The Beastman eyes them carefully and acknowledges their respect. He may be wary, but it seems he is not going to attack them.

To their surprise, he points toward a plateau on the mountain, where Eenali and his tribesmen can stay in premade huts. He also displays his generous nature by handing the injured tribesman a cup of liquid.

"Drink this and you'll be healed in five days," he says. "And apply this to your wound. It counters the poison," he adds.

The injured tribesman nods meekly. The others are in awe of his kindness. He also provides Eenali's team a mixture of herbs[25] whose aroma helps the tribesmen recover from their altitude sickness.

He is deadly and fierce, yet kind and compassionate, marvels Eenali. "This in itself is the greatest lesson we can learn," he thinks.

After staying there for several days, Eenali becomes restless. He feels that the Beastman who initially looked helpful might be more private than Eenali had assumed. He is almost ready to sneak into the cave and uncover any knowledge Beastman might be safeguarding. After losing his wife, Eenali's outlook on life has become more bitter. She was the source of calmness as well as the voice of reason for him. There was a time when Eenali was unsure if his elder son Emla was interested in laying claim to the title of tribe successor. Eenali's wife had told him to wait for the right moment and gave him the wisdom of how to handle the situation. "If you never ask you never know," she had said. Her lesson was perhaps equally applicable to the current situation, wondered Eenali.

---

[25] Camphor, Eucalyptus leaves and Cloves

He changes his mind and decides to formally meet the Beastman again and explain why they took the trouble to embark on this treacherous journey. He finally gathers the courage to enter the castle with two of his men. Although the Beastman may not have spoken about the ugly incident, Eenali believes that it is his duty to apologize.

Eenali bows to the Beastman and says, "Greetings, my lord! First of all, I want to apologize for the unsavory incident involving one of our men. I take full responsibility for it. If you've thought of a punishment, please direct it to me, as I was supposed to lead my men, in which I failed."

"It's not your mistake," the Beastman responds. "He must learn to control his urges. Men from successful tribes never force a woman like that," he continues, with a flash of anger in his eyes.

"I'm very sorry, my Lord. I will make sure that it never happens again. Please forgive us," Eenali answers, folding his hands. He knows that he must ask for forgiveness. It is a miracle that they are all still alive.

The Beastman nods and asks him to continue.

"We have come from far to seek knowledge that may help us sustain our tribe. We have faced repeated attacks from outsiders, and our tribe has undergone drastic attrition. What was once a thriving group of over fifty people is now reduced to barely ten," he says, with sorrow constricting his throat.

Forcing himself to continue, he adds, "The benevolent Fireman taught us the art of preserving fire and making weapons. He shared the secrets of fire, water, and earth. Yet, he said that to truly thrive, we should seek your blessings."

The Beastman ponders over Eenali's words. Making up his mind that he must help them, he gestures toward a cliff and orders him to follow him. Eenali does as commanded.

"Sit down," he says, pointing at a rock. Eenali immediately obeys. He is hopeful that the Beastman may be open to sharing some skills and knowledge. Unknown to the tribesmen, the Fireman and Beastman have known each other for decades and share great camaraderie and mutual respect.

"The greatest power is the power of numbers," the Beastman says. He draws a biconvex symbol that looks like a vertical slit on a rock using a chalk stone.

"But do you know how we get numbers?" he asks, testing Eenali. Eenali knows that the Beastman is asking how men and women reproduce. He racks his brain, pondering how to answer the question.

Eenali, like everyone else, believes that babies are born when a man and woman are together. It is just a natural process, according to him and his kin. Just as more watering facilitates the sprouts to grow from a seed into a sapling, a man spending more intimate time with a fertile woman is likely to increase the chances of the woman giving birth. Eenali's understanding of the biology of reproduction is actually greater than what most of the humans know in this era. The connection between intercourse and childbirth is not so obvious to most since the two are separated by a duration of many months.

The Beastman waits patiently as Eenali tries to form sentences with what little he knows. Deep inside, the Beastman is aware that Eenali is ignorant like the rest of them. It has taken the Beastman years of close observation of various species and careful deductive skills to reach the conclusion that he is about to share with Eenali.

Once it becomes clear that Eenali has no answer, the Beastman draws four crescents in a series. Then, he draws the same biconvex symbol below every crescent. Eenali realizes that the crescent is the symbol of the moon and that the Beastman is indicating a time period of one moon cycle or twenty-eight days between each moon.

The Beastman then makes a nick in his thumb and drops several drops of blood on the biconvex symbols. Eenali watches mutely as the Beastman takes a smooth, elongated black pebble from his bag and touches that pebble at three points, precisely in the middle of the two biconvex symbols.

This was it: the secret of life. So simple yet so powerful that it can change the course of the human race. Eenali, being the experienced and learned man that he is, immediately understands the message. If men and women come together in the middle of the cycles, it greatly increases the chances of women conceiving. This is how he can repopulate his village. Eenali's eyes tear up, and he thanks the Beastman profusely. In turn, the Beastman gives Eenali the black pebble as a souvenir and reminder of the important lesson that he has learned.

The Beastman is happy with Eenali's intelligence. He is quick to learn and even quicker to show respect. He decides to impart more knowledge during the remainder of their stay.

For the next several days, the tribe stays in the huts and closely observes the activities of the Beastman and his consort. They are deft in interacting with herds of animals, including sheep, cows, horses, yaks, and even birds. Tribesmen are struck by how the Beastman communicates with animals and manages them easily. Even smaller wild animals, such as mountain wolves, listen to him and follow his commands.

However, the Beastman goes hunting for larger predators such as mountain lions, snow tigers, and bears. The Beastman is strong enough to slay the most sizable predators and hands their skins around to those who live in the mountains where he resides. Across thousands of miles of mountains, as far as the eyes can see, the Beastman is the ruler, serving both as a guardian and apex predator.

The tribe also learns how to identify non-poisonous snakes.

This is a great lesson for Eenali and his tribe since many of their people have previously succumbed to snakes. For the common man, it is impossible to distinguish between a harmless and a poisonous snake.

Eenali thanks the Beastman once more silently, for he will be saving the lives of many of his tribe members in the future. He also realizes that they now have an edge over others. They can use non-venomous snakes as a scare tactic while being assured that they are not deadly.

Lastly, the Beastman teaches a select few how to handle poisonous snakes and extract their venom without harming them to increase the lethality of their arrowheads and spikes.

Eenali notes that despite all the rage and ferocity inside, the Beastman is a remarkably disciplined man. He is up bright and early every morning before others. Before the first rays of the sun caress the tops of the mountain, he is ready to face the world. Additionally, his posture is erect and rigid, and he meditates every morning. Then, he performs a specific set of stretching exercises[26] every day. This is the secret to his agility and remarkable strength.

Despite all of his power, they never once see the Beastman become angry without reason. Never does he mistreat weaker men and women. Although he is popular and can have any woman he desires, he never abuses his authority. His eyes and love are meant only for his consort, with whom he has a son.

____

[26] Yoga

Eenali and his tribesmen are learning what it means to be strong, yet civilized, and this experience will leave a lasting impression on all of the men and women and shape the culture of their tribe for many generations to come.

One morning, a member of Eenali's tribe sees a beautiful zebu calf. Being particularly hungry that day, he thinks of killing and eating the calf. He slowly walks closer to the animal and takes out a sharp knife, stabbing the calf in its neck. The calf screams frantically, calling for its mother. Other cows of the herd cry in pain, distressed to see their young one helpless. He then moves forward to cut a bigger artery and kill the calf, making plans about how he's going to enjoy its tender meat.

The tribesman lunges forward, but a spear comes flying out of nowhere and cuts his forearm. He cries in agony and clutches his arm, only to see the Beastman standing next to him, his eyes as black as smoldering coals staring at him, ready to cut his head off with his tri-point spear. Eenali hears the commotion and intervenes. He has already lost too many of his men and does not want to lose another. He drops down to the Beastman's knees and begs for forgiveness.

"Hunger has got the best of him, my lord," he pleads. "It has been a difficult journey for all of us. Please spare him this one time, for you are as gentle and forgiving as you are strong and fierce."

The Beastman stares at Eenali, his anger subsiding a little. He reasons that the man who struck the calf is a fool but killing him will not teach him anything.

"Your men have no knowledge of animals or nature. All you can think of is food - selfish and brute," he roars, addressing the wounded man in particular. "I will forgive you and spare your life, but there's one condition," he adds. "You and your likes will sit with me to enhance your understanding of the animal kingdom. You will benefit much more by being friends with them rather than killing them every time you see an opportunity," he says and walks away.

Eenali frantically applies pressure to the wounded forearm and succeeds in stopping the bleeding. Later that day, Beastman's consort sutures the wound to help the injured man heal faster. Eenali and his men are sorry for their acts, but they realize that this is how they have always acted. They only know to hunt and kill, since food has been scarce. They hope that the Beastman can forgive them and teach them something valuable.

The next day, Eenali and his men appear in front of the Beastman and his consort. The consort takes chalk and explains to the tribe that the animal kingdom is divided into two parts. First, there are those that need to be protected; the *dociles* are peace-loving animals that generally depend on plants or small insects for their food. Then, there are those from which we should protect ourselves; these are the *Wilds*, which are aggressive carnivores who are not only threats to humans, but also to plant-eating animals. Man, being at the top of this chain, has the option to take some of these animals as his food.

The wild ones are difficult to catch, but they can serve as food in dire situations. The docile ones are the easiest to catch and are suitable for human consumption, including children. However, not all docile animals should be killed. Among them, there are some that are *gifted*. The gifted ones have certain abilities that make them more suitable for very specific purposes.

These animals include horses, which are among the fastest animals and capable of treading all types of terrains. Then, there is the elephant, which is difficult to befriend; however, if cared for since infancy, they can prove to be the most powerful weightlifter, trawler, and defender. Finally, there is the *supremely gifted* - cow.

The Beastman then joins the group with the calf that was stabbed by Eenali's tribesman. The Beastman has sutured the calf's lacerations and given it some delicious herbs to help it heal.

"The cow is the only animal that can care for others and has the compassion to match evolved beings like humans," he says. "It will also happily share its milk with anyone it cares for. Furthermore, cow's milk is the only milk that is rich enough to heal even the most wounded warrior, yet gentle enough for even a newborn baby to digest. I know many tribes that lost their women during childbirth but were able to sustain their newborns and young ones on cow's milk for years until they became strong enough to fetch and eat for themselves," he adds, while indicating his consort to continue.

"You had asked us what makes the difference between a successful tribe that can sustain itself for decades and become stronger with each generation, and a tribe that succumbs to adversities and vanishes under the tides of time," the consort says. "Here is your answer. These zebu cows produce exceptional milk that can sustain the old and young. The fatty precipitate is ideal for cooking oil or lighting lamps, their dried dung can help sustain fire, and the bulls are great for farming."

Once again, Eenali feels enlightened and thanks the Beastman and his consort. The Beastman also gifts them a horse, which Eenali will himself command. However, it is now time to leave, and they bid goodbye to the Beastman and his consort after thanking them one final time.

One day after leaving the mountains, their tribe comes under attack from five clansmen of a barbaric tribe from the North. Eenali knows that his tribe is already at its weakest and cannot survive the attack. As a last resort, he blows the whistle that the Lady of the Lake had given him in the hope that someone might hear it and come to help.

To Eenali's surprise, someone does, in fact, come. It is none other than the Beastman himself. The leader of the attacking squad is instantly killed by an arrow shot from the Beastman's longbow. Then, he throws two wooden bottles that explode with poisonous smoke and briefly incapacitates the attackers. The swiftness with which the Beastman moves, attacks, and dodges the attacks on him is nothing less than magic. It looks as if he is executing some

exquisite dance moves that he has created and mastered after years of practice. His long bow and tri-point spear are extensions of his body. Within five minutes, he has single-handedly killed all five attackers.

The Beastman warns Eenali that the attackers were just scouts. In his experience, these small attacks are always followed by waves of attacks by armies of Northern barbaric tribes coming down the slopes. It will be best for Eenali to leave quickly. The Beastman gives him two longbows to help them protect their entourage.

The Beastman takes a final glance at Eenali's tribe, or what is left of it, and says to himself, "there is no way this tribe can sustain the long journey back to the Western drylands." He takes a deep breath and tells Eenali, "There is a place where the food is plentiful, water is pure, air is clean, and earth is teeming with life. *The Wiseman* is the only one who can guide you to that promised land. Follow this stream until the snow melts and the water changes color, and you shall meet him. He is the all-knowing who watches all four directions at once. He is so wise that he knows the past, present, and future. If you can seek his blessings, it will give your tribe a true chance to thrive. Good luck!"

Chapter 9
The Blind Guide

तत सूर्यस्य देवत्वं तन महित्वं मध्या कर्तोर्विततं सं जभार |
यदेदयुक्त हरितः सधस्थादाद रात्री वासस्तनुते सिमस्मै ||

This is the Godhead, this might of Surya: he hath withdrawn

what spread over work unfinished.

When he hath loosed his horses from their station, straight

over all night spreadeth out its garment.

(Rigveda 01:115:04)

Eenali's tribe follows the river for three days before they reach a similar stream where darker water meets theirs. The Beastman had said that the water will change its color, which means that they have reached their destination. After receiving guidance from a nearby village, Eenali realizes that he has reached the correct place, except that he is not the only one. Many other men and women are also waiting in anticipation of talking to the Wiseman. One of whom is Kiki.

The Wiseman is perched under a dense tree, his abode is in the nearby cave. His skin is pale due to a lack of sun exposure. He has a thick white beard and looks twice as old as the oldest man Kiki had ever seen. Upon closer examination, Kiki notices that the black of his eye has turned completely white.

As the men take a good look at the Wiseman, they also assess one another. Kiki and Eenali see each other for the first time. As leaders of their respective tribes, they acknowledge each other with respect. Even though they speak different languages, wear different clothes, and pray to different deities, they are both victims of destiny. Their adversity, determination, and quest for redemption are strong enough to unite them.

Eenali gestures toward the Wiseman's crown and bobs his eyebrows, asking a silent question. Kiki instantly understands that Eenali is asking about the strange-looking crown that the Wiseman is wearing. Kiki points his two fingers to his own eyes, indicating that the Wiseman is perhaps blind. Incredibly, they understand each other without uttering a word.

On their way, both Kiki and Eenali have heard more than their share of stories floating about the Wiseman. People say that he is so old that he has traveled all over the world. After imbibing all of the world's knowledge and wisdom, his eyes finally gave up and he went blind.

The Wiseman wears a crown with three artificial human-like heads that give the impression that he is seeing in all four directions so that predators do not sneak up on him from any side. It is said that his masked crown was gifted to him by the Fireman from the West. Even the weapons of the men guarding the Wiseman's cave look similar to the weapons that Eenali saw in the Fireman's castle. People say that these sentries are some of the finest in all of the Himalayas and were trained by none other than the mightiest warrior, the Beastman himself.

Finally, it is Kiki's turn to approach the Wiseman. The stairs leading to him are brimming with beautiful lotus flowers on both sides. Kiki is nervous. He has traveled very far and faced numerous dangers just to get to this brief moment. He finally reaches the topmost step, which leads to a large flat platform, where the Wiseman sits beneath a very old giant banyan tree. There are some other tribesmen who have also traveled from afar and are currently seated on the ground next to the platform where Wiseman is.

Kiki explains as best as he can with his language and gestures that he comes from the South. His village has been decimated by diseases and plagues. Despite inhabiting those areas for centuries, his village has never been able to grow as quickly as he and other elders had hoped for. To his surprise, the Wiseman seems to understand everything he says. He does have some minimal vision and is not completely blind.

Finally, Kiki hears a deep voice saying, "You are trying to get ahead of time. Never try to get ahead of time." Kiki is puzzled. The Wiseman continues, "Where you live may appear to be a great location, but it is not yet ripe for growth. One day, humanity will advance enough that your troubles will become mere history, but now is not that time. If you and others like you want to grow and prosper, you need to follow the River of Life. It will take you through the marshes and lead you to the most beautiful and surreal plains you can imagine, where the food is plentiful, the land is giving, and diseases are scarce. It is protected from all directions. But first, I must know that you are worthy of this knowledge. You can sit here and join the rest of them." He points at the others waiting patiently. Kiki goes to the side and joins the rest of the men. He is more confused than ever but ponders over what the Wiseman has said.

After several hours, many other men and women come and seek the Wiseman's guidance. Many receive their answers, thank the Wiseman, and return happy and contented. However, the crowd of villagers sitting with Kiki swells to over twenty. Eenali has also joined this crowd by now. Again, Kiki and Eenali look at each other with silent questions writ large on their faces. They realize they are close to achieving what they have come for, yet it feels elusive and distant.

As the sun is setting, the sentries close the community gathering and the Wiseman turns to this flock of villagers. "Oh, villagers! If your village has an abundance of food and water, absence of diseases as well as good defenses against enemies, what else do you need to prosper?" he asks. The audience is perplexed. If they have food, water, and protection from diseases and enemies, what more could anyone ask for?

Then, Kiki and Eenali stand up and say in unison, "Traditions."

The Wiseman smiles. This is exactly the answer that he was looking for. He has witnessed hundreds of villages and tribes rise and fall. Almost every community, regardless of how strong they think they are, eventually perishes to the tides of time. That is unless they have understood the true secret to success.

The knowledge in this world is too vast for anyone to grasp in one lifetime. Unless a community comes up with the means to pass on its knowledge very accurately to the next generation, the overall strength of the community will never increase. That is why traditions are important. Passing on hard-earned knowledge and skills in a rigorous manner to the next generation for them to build upon is the real secret that very few men and women understand.

The Wiseman is satisfied with Eenali and Kiki. He sends the rest of the men away and asks Eenali and Kiki to come forward. After everyone else leaves the area, he takes them both to a precipice from which they can see hundreds of miles into the distance. He shows them a specific stream of water: it is a tributary of the majestic River Ganga.

Chapter 10
River of Life

इमं मे गङ्गे यमुने सरस्वति शुतुद्रि स्तेमं सचता परुष्ण्या।
असिक्न्या मरुद्वृधे वितस्तयार्जीकीये शृणुह्यासुषोमया॥

Favour ye this my lord, O Ganga, Yamuna, O Sutudri, Parusni

and Sarasvati: With Asikni, Vitasta, O Marudvrdha, O Arjikiya

with Susoma hear my call.

(Rigveda 10:075:05)

During the week that Eenali and Kiki spend near Wiseman's abode, he shares vital knowledge with them.

He directs his sentries to teach Eenali and Kiki's tribesmen how to use oil from the *Neem*[27] tree to protect themselves from parasites and burn neem leaves to repel mosquitoes. He also demonstrates how *Neem* and *Tulsi*[28] can be used to purify water prior to drinking it, thus reducing the risk of stomach infections.

"Men in these mountains have utilized *Neem* oil for ages now," he says. "It is not wrong to say that it is magical. You can even use it to drive pests away from your crops. However, use it in moderation, as too much of any one thing is bad," he cautions.

Kiki and Eenali nod their heads, absorbing everything that the Wiseman says. Their confidence grows with every word. Finally, they can hope to present some type of deterrence from parasites to their tribes.

On the day of their departure, the Wiseman gives them a sacred herb to treat marsh fever. He cautions them to take it in a specific amount over one full moon cycle. He personally teaches them how to identify the source plant[29] in the wild. He then shows them how to prepare

---

[27] Azadirachta Indica

[28] Holy basil

[29] Artemisia

Trifala, a mixture of three potent herbs: *Amalaka,*[30] *Bibhitaki,*[31] and *Haritaki,*[32] which will cure yellow fever.

Finally, he demonstrates how to process the urine from a pregnant cow to produce a protein-rich potion that can provide energy to patients debilitated by chronic diseases, such as Black Death and Yakshma, and save their lives.

The Wiseman also informs them that bovine urine can be used as fertilizer for crops. "You see, you do not need much to make the plants grow. Just mix this in equal amounts of water, and Mother Earth will take care of the rest."

Both Kiki and Eenali thank the Wiseman for sharing such precious knowledge. The Wiseman wishes them good luck on their journey.

But that was half a moon ago.

Two weeks have passed since the Wiseman showed Eenali and Kiki the way to the mystic plains that were the answer to their problems. Kiki and Eenali have now united their tribesmen, and together, they are much stronger than before. They have realized that strength lies not only in passing knowledge, but in standing united as well.

At first, Kiki was skeptical about following the river

----

[30] Emblica officinalis

[31] Terminalia bellerica

[32] Terminalia chebula

because it entailed walking through the marshes, and he fears Marsh Fever. He and his men have already endured a lot, and his primary aim is to return home and share his precious knowledge with his tribesmen. After all, what is the point of their suffering if they cannot even pass on what they learned? What if they perish before they return? Anxiety torments him, but he does not dare question the Wiseman. He has reasons to believe that every word spoken by Wiseman must be right. Two nights before the tribe's departure, the Wiseman had told all of them to dip their footwear in a special tree sap.[33] The sap hardened over the next few days turning their ordinary foot covering to water-resistant footwear with flexible soles. If it was not for this enhancement, the two tribes would have succumbed to the dangerous Himalayan terrain.[34] Their group has managed to survive through dense forests and marshes using the techniques taught by the Wiseman. As a farewell gift, the wiseman had handed them a box containing ten medicinal plant seeds including *Shatavari*[35] and *Aragvadha*[36], which can be used to heal women after childbirth. The box also contained detailed drawings of medicinal plants like *Nitya Pushpa*[37] and Happy tree for treatment of

---

[33] Ficus elastica

[34] Garhwal region

[35] Asparagus Racemosus

[36] Cassia Fistula

[37] Catharanthus roseus

Raktajwar and tumors; and *Vidanga*[38] for treatment of internal parasites.

However, plagued with hunger, fatigue, and a mixture of anger and irritation, their desperation is reaching its limit now. Some tribesmen have even attempted to rebel against their tribe leaders, fearing that they may have lost their way. Nevertheless, Kiki and Eenali know that the Wiseman is no fraud. The skills that he taught them are so powerful that their group is able to cruise through one of the densest forests that they have ever encountered.

After two more days of walking, the group reaches the edge of the modern-day Shivalik Forest. In front of them is the majestic view of a mountain range breaking in the middle, as if creating a doorway to offer them a glimpse of the fabled plains of Ganga. The entourage is elated to glimpse the lush green plains. Emla is so ecstatic that his crutch drops from his hands in excitement. Before he can lose balance and fall, Nira holds his arms and stabilizes him. "I might know some exercises that can help you heal faster," she says. Struck by the beautiful eyes of his helper, Emla is at a loss for words, but manages to smile back and thank her.

With this, their journey has finally come to an end. Over the next several months, both Kiki and Eenali send

---

[38] Embelia ribes

messengers to their respective tribes and trusted allies, directing them to follow the path and unite in the Great Gangetic Plains.

The dream of a glorious Gangetic civilization that the Fireman, Beastman, and Wiseman had envisioned many decades ago was getting closer to realization. After years of patiently waiting and some strokes of luck, a group of diligent and honorable men and women finally began to unite in the Great Plains.

Every long journey begins with a single step, and this was the step that would lead to everything that followed since. All of the wheels had been set in motion. And thus, it began…

About the author

Suraj Pratap is a Pediatric Hematologist and Oncologist who lives with his family in Las Vegas. Born in Madhepura and raised in Ahmedabad, Suraj has traveled extensively throughout India. Subsequently, his training and education took him to the USA and Europe where he continued his study of the latest advances in the field of medicine and cancer research. Despite his travels across the globe, his connections with India have remained steadfast. He used all opportunities he could get to travel to religious sites throughout India and Nepal. These religious journeys not only enhanced his understanding of ancient Hindu traditions and lore, but also evoked his interest in trying to understand how some of these ancient legends may have originated. This book is an attempt to condense some of those ideas in the form of a fictitious tale. The author hopes that this book will enrich the reader's imagination and generate healthy discussions that can lead to a better appreciation of Hindu mythology.